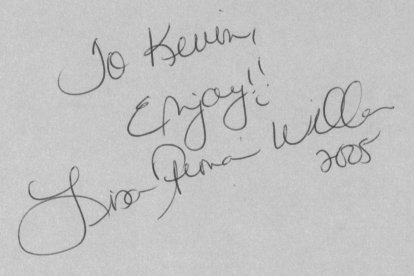

To Kevin,
Enjoy!!
Lisa Perma Wills
2005

Where Do Snowmen Go?

Written by Lisa Funari Willever

Illustrations by Chris Gash

Franklin Mason Press
Trenton, New Jersey

For Jessica and Patrick, *always believe....LFW*

For Skylar, who so effortlessly restored my faith in love at first sight and to Elwood and Harvey, for the inspiration and the late night company...CG

The editors at Franklin Mason Press would like to thank those who graciously serve on the Guest Young Author and Guest Young Illustrator committees. Your care in selecting the work of young writers and artists today will help to shape and inspire the authors and illustrators of tomorrow.

Text copyright © Lisa Funari Willever, 2002

Illustration Copyright © Chris Gash, 2002

Cover and interior design by Peri Poloni, Knockout Design, Cameron Park, CA – www.knockoutbooks.com.

Editorial Staff: Marcia Jacobs, Linda Funari, and Catherine Funari

Published in the United States – Printed in Singapore

10 9 8 7 6 5 4 3 2

Franklin Mason Press ISBN No. 0-9679227-2-0
Library of Congress Control Number: 2002109705

Other Franklin Mason Press titles by Lisa Funari Willever

Everybody Moos At Cows
The Easter Chicken
Chumpkin
Maximilian The Great
You Can't Walk A Fish
On Your Mark, Get Set, Teach!

Franklin Mason press is proud to support the important work of the Sunshine Foundation. In that spirit, $0.25 will be donated from the sale of each book. To learn more about their work, see our About the Charity page at the end of the book or visit **www.franklinmasonpress.com.**

Each year we build a snowman,
when the first flakes start to fall.

A snowman in a baseball cap,
standing six feet tall.

But the snowman that we built this year was different than the rest.

He was special in a kind of way we never could have guessed.

And even though he's made of snow and frozen through and through,

he soon became our new best friend, and so we named him Lou.

We watched Lou through our window, as he stood in our front yard.

In our imaginary castle, he became the Palace Guard.

We told him all our secrets, though he never said a word.

We told him that we loved him and somehow our Lou heard.

We knew that spring was coming quick, the air was not too chilly.

We wished that we could drive him North, but that would just be silly.

Tonight we didn't fall asleep, we tried hard not to cry.

Knowing that our Lou would melt, we went to say, "Good-bye."

We crept out to the front yard, before the morning sun

and a voice we never heard before said, "Thanks, it's sure been fun!"

We looked at one another and then we looked at Lou.

That night our snowman spoke to us, it's strange but it is true.

"Why do you two look so glum? Why the sad long faces?

I'll miss you both, but I must go and visit other places."

We never knew that he could speak, we thought he was just snow.

But since he could, we had to ask...

"WHERE DO SNOWMEN GO?"

"When the air begins to warm up and winter starts to fade,

we slip out on a moonlit night and make our own parade.

One by one, we join the line, on frozen tip-toe feet,

careful not to make a sound as we walk down the street."

"Light and quick,
sometimes we walk, other
times we fly.

We disguise ourselves as
puffy clouds and float up
in the sky.

Looking for some action,
then some rest and relaxation,

once we're loved we never melt
...*we just go on* VACATION!"

"We hula in Hawaii,
to lose a little weight.

We stop by San Francisco, to
stroll the Golden Gate.

We visit New York City, New
Zealand, France, and Rome,

'til our reservation's ready at
our *home away from home.*"

"On an island near the South Pole, there's a town called Mt. Retreat,

where snowmen come from near and far, to just get off their feet.

With hotels standing 10 floors high, made of solid ice,

close enough to touch the stars...a snowman's paradise."

"We paint like Michelangelo, on ceilings made of snow.

We dress up in tuxedos for an off, off Broadway show.

There's shuffleboard and tennis, there's a party every night.

We mamba and we samba underneath the pale moonlight."

We hugged our Lou and waved good-bye, but never went to bed.

We hid outside and there it was, just like our Lou said,

One by one, the snowmen, who stood along our street,

joined the line of snowmen, marching by on tip-toe feet.

And underneath the street light, written in the melting snow,

Was a message from our dear friend Lou, we spotted down below:

"Anything that's built with love, becomes quite real it's said.

I'll see you both next year, now get inside and GO TO BED!"

ANYTHING BUILT
THAT'S BUILT
WITH

"Peterson The Mouse"

by Alexander Mckenzie

Age 6 Brick, NJ—Veterans Memorial Elementary School

ONCE THERE WAS A MOUSE NAMED PETERSON. Peterson was a small, brown mouse. He had a white tummy, a pointy nose, and he was very, very smart.

One day he was hungry for cheese. He smelled cheese and followed the smell to a big white house. He knew the cheese was inside, but he saw a big, furry, white cat. He thought and he thought. He needed to find a way to trick the cat into going outside.

Peterson knocked on the door, then stepped to the side, out of sight. The cat opened the door and saw a wind-up mouse. The cat chased the toy mouse into the front yard and Peterson quickly snuck inside and locked the cat out. He searched all of the rooms for the cheese. The smell was strongest in the kitchen. He saw the cheese on a plate and climbed up onto the table. He ate the cheese and laughed while the cat kept meowing and ringing the doorbell!

"The Ballerina's Slippers

by Maryrose DiPierro

Age 8 Hamilton, NJ – Robinson Elementary School

ONCE THERE WAS A BALLERINA DOLL NAMED CLARA. She was pretty and she wore a tutu that was pink. She lived in a doll shop. Nobody bought her because she was missing slippers.

One night, the girl begged her mother to get the ballerina doll. The next morning, after all of the begging, her mother agreed to let her get the doll. She ran to the doll shop to buy Clara the Ballerina Doll.

She took Clara home with her and even made her slippers. When she slipped them on, the doll came alive. The girl asked the doll what her name was and the doll said, "Lindsay!"

Snooze The Ducky Is Very Sad

By Brianna Cannizzo

Age 6 Deer Park, NY – May Moore Elementary School

SNOOZE THE DUCKY WAS FEELING VERY SAD TODAY. He was bored. But then he got an idea! He would sit down and roll the ball with his friends. When Snooze asked his friends if they would roll the ball with him, they said, "No." When he asked his other friends to roll the ball, they also said, "No." This made Snooze really sad again and he started to cry.

Later, Snooze asked his friends to have a picnic and they still said, "No." Snooze started to cry again. His friends were sorry to make him cry, but they still said, "No." As Snooze was crying, his friends found him and said, "Come with us." When he got there, he saw that his friends had thrown him a surprise party! Now, Snooze the Ducky is very happy.

Guest Young Illustrator

"Portrait With Teddy Roosevelt"

Gianni Napolitano
Age 9 East Norwich, NY
James Vernon School

"You Can Walk A Fish"

Rebecca Margolis
Age 9 Linwood, NJ
Seaview Avenue Elementary School

"My Great Dane"

Alexis Wansac
Age 9 Wellington, FL
Panther Run Elementary School

FRANKLIN MASON PRESS is looking for stories and illustrations from children 6-9 years old to appear in our books. We are dedicated to providing children with an avenue into the world of publishing.

If you would like to be our next Guest Young Author or Guest Young Illustrator, read the information below and send us your work.

To be a Guest Young Author:

Send us a 75-200 word story about something strange, funny, or unusual. Stories may be fiction or non-fiction. Be sure to follow the rules below.

To be a Guest Young Illustrator:

Draw a picture using crayons, markers, or colored pencils. Do not write words on your picture and be sure to follow the rules below.

Prizes

1st Place Author / 1st Place Illustrator

$25.00, a framed award, a complimentary book and your work will be published in FMP's newest book.

2nd Place Author / 2nd Place Illustrator

$15.00, a framed award, a complimentary book and your work will be published in FMP's newest book.

3rd Place Author / 3rd Place Illustrator

$10.00, a framed award, a complimentary book and your work will be published in FMP's newest book.

Rules For The Contest

1. Children may enter one category only, either Author or Illustrator.
2. All stories must be typed or written very neatly.
3. All illustrations should be on 8.5" x 11" paper and must be sent in between 2 pieces of cardboard to prevent wrinkling.
4. Name, address, phone number, school, and parent's signature must be on the back of all submissions.
5. All work must be original and completed solely by the child.
6. Franklin Mason Press reserves the right to print submitted material. All work becomes property of FMP and will not be returned. Any work selected is considered a work for hire and FMP will retain all rights.
7. There is no deadline for submissions. FMP will publish children's work in every book published. All submissions are considered for the most current title.
8. All submissions should be sent to:

> Youth Submissions Editor, Franklin Mason Press
> P.O. Box 3808, Trenton, NJ 08629
> **www.franklinmasonpress.com**

Tips for Young Authors & Illustrators

1. Write and draw about things you enjoy. If you need an idea, think of your family, your friends, or your favorite things to do.

2. Find a nice quiet place where you can write or draw.

3. If you are having trouble making up your story, make a list of ideas that you want to write about. Use your list to get started.

4. If you become stuck in the middle of a story, put it away and go back to it the next day. Sometimes all you need is to take a break or get some rest.

5. Remember, your first draft of a story is never your last draft! Rewrite, rewrite, rewrite....until it's perfect.

6. When proofreading your work, *read each line backwards* to find spelling errors.

7. Share your stories and illustrations with your friends, family, and teachers.

8. If you are between the ages of 6-9 years old, send your work to Franklin Mason Press...Home of the Guest Young Author and Illustrator Contest!

For ideas and activities for Young Authors and Illustrators, visit
www.franklinmasonpress.com

About The Sunshine Foundation

FOR SIX YEARS WILLIAM SAMPLE, a 40 year old police officer, had been assigned to protective duty at St. Christopher's Hospital for Children in Philadelphia. Among the patients were a large number of chronically or terminally ill children. Over the years, Sample came to know many of the children and, as well, families who had been drained financially and emotionally. He wished that he could do something to ease their suffering.

From this desire, the Sunshine Foundation was formed over twenty years ago. Sunshine's mission is to answer the dreams and wishes of suffering children. Whether the dream is a visit with a celebrity hero, a family outing, or a trip to Disney World, the foundation has granted over 26,500 dreams to children ages 3 to 21 with an endless list of diseases and disabilities. And Sunshine is one of the few wish-granting organizations that makes dreams come true for chronically ill children, as well as terminally ill children.

Franklin Mason Press is pleased to support the wonderful work of Bill Sample and the Sunshine Foundation. For more information, please visit www.sunshinefoundation.org.

SINCE 1976

About the Author & Illustrator

Lisa Funari Willever (author) is a lifelong resident of Trenton, New Jersey and a former teacher in the Trenton Public School District. She is a graduate of The College of New Jersey (formerly Trenton State College) and a past member of the National Education Association, the New Jersey Education Association, and the New Jersey Reading Association. She is also the author of several children's books: *You Can't Walk A Fish, The Culprit Was A Fly, Miracle On Theodore's Street, Maximilian The Great, The Easter Chicken,* and *Everybody Moos At Cows* as well as *On Your Mark, Get Set, Teach – The Must Have Guide For New Teachers.* Her husband, Todd, is a professional Firefighter in the city of Trenton, N.J. and the co-author of *Miracle on Theodore's Street.* They are the proud parents of three year old Jessica and two year old Patrick.

Chris Gash (illustrator) is a freelance illustrator. His drawings appear regularly in the New York Times, the Wall Street Journal, and the Washington Post. He works late nights in Montclair, New Jersey.

About Franklin Mason Press

Franklin Mason Press was founded in Trenton, New Jersey in September 1999. While our main goal is to produce quality reading materials, we also provide children with an avenue into the world of publishing. Our Guest Young Author and Illustrator Contest offers children an opportunity to submit their work and possibly become published authors and illustrators. In addition, Franklin Mason Press is proud to support children's charities with donations from book sales. Each new children's title benefits a different children's charity. For more information, please visit

www.franklinmasonpress.com

Franklin Mason Press

PO Box 3808 Trenton, New Jersey 08629